Here are some other Redfeather Books you will enjoy

The Curse of the Trouble Dolls
by Dian Curtis Regan

Lavender
by Karen Hesse

Max Malone the Magnificent
by Charlotte Herman

A Moon in Your Lunch Box
by Michael Spooner

The Peppermint Race
by Dian Curtis Regan

The Riddle Streak
by Susan Beth Pfeffer

Sable
by Karen Hesse

Snakes Are Nothing to Sneeze At
by Gabrielle Charbonnet

Tutu Much Ballet
by Gabrielle Charbonnet

Twin Surprises
by Susan Beth Pfeffer

Twin Troubles
by Susan Beth Pfeffer

Weird Wolf
by Margery Cuyler

*Available in paperback

Pedro Fools the Gringo

And Other Tales of a Latin American Trickster

FOOLS THE GRINGO
And Other Tales of a
Latin American Trickster

• • •

María Cristina Brusca and Tona Wilson
Illustrated by María Cristina Brusca

A Redfeather Book
Henry Holt and Company • New York

Henry Holt and Company, Inc.
Publishers since 1866
115 West 18th Street
New York, New York 10011

Henry Holt is a registered
trademark of Henry Holt and Company, Inc.

Published in Canada by Fitzhenry & Whiteside Ltd.,
195 Allstate Parkway, Markham, Ontario L3R 4T8.

Library of Congress Cataloging-in-Publication Data
Brusca, María Cristina.
Pedro fools the gringo and other tales of a Latin American
trickster / by María Cristina Brusca and Tona Wilson;
illustrated by María Cristina Brusca.
p.   cm.—(A Redfeather Book)
"Where the stories come from:" —p.
Includes bibliographical references (p.   ).
Contents: Clever little Pedro—Painted horses—The golden partridge—
The magic pot—The money tree—Pig tails in the swamp—
The helper rabbit—Burro gold—Pedro and the devil—
Pedro fools the gringo—"Good-bye to your machetes . . ."—
Pedro goes to heaven.
1. Tales—Latin America.   2. Children's stories, Latin American.
[1. Folklore—Latin America.   2. Trickster—Folklore.   3. Short stories.]
I. Wilson, Tona.   II. Title.   III. Series: Redfeather books.
PZ8.1.B8374Pe   1995   [398.2]—dc20   95-9984

ISBN 0-8050-3827-2

First Edition—1995

Printed in the United States of America
on acid-free paper. ∞
1   3   5   7   9   10   8   6   4   2

To Mark Sovocool

Contents

Pedro Fools the Gringo

And Other Tales of a Latin American Trickster

Introduction

"I heard this a long time ago, and I'm not sure if it's true or not. . . ." a storyteller begins. The story is about Pedro Urdemales, the trickster. The name *Urdemales* means something like "weaver of evil" in Spanish, but it is not really evil that Pedro plots; it is his own survival. Down to his last few cents as the story begins, he waits for the chance to match his wits against someone else's greed and foolishness. And by the end of the story we can be sure that Pedro will have gotten what he wanted, at the expense of his adversaries.

Pedro Urdemales has been around for a long time. The first recorded mention of Pedro Urdemales comes from Spain in the 1100s, and the name appeared frequently in Spanish literature in the fifteenth century. Some of his exploits are similar to picaresque stories—adventure tales with roguish heroes—in Spanish literature. And a Pedro de Urdemalas is the protagonist of a play by Cervantes.

But Pedro's origins are solidly in the oral storytelling tradition. His exploits have been told in Spain for hundreds of years. When the Spanish came to the Americas, Pedro Urdemales came with them. He thrived, and was known by many names, among them Pedro Tecomate ("Peter Gourd"), Pedro de Malas ("Peter Wickedness"), Pedro Malasartes ("Peter Evilarts"), and Juan de Urdimales ("John Evilschemer"). Stories, jokes, and anecdotes about these characters are told not only in Spanish but in Aymara, a language spoken by descendants of the Inca in Bolivia and Peru; in the Mayan languages of Guatemala and Mexico; in English, in the southwestern United States; and in other languages.

The people Pedro dupes are generally the rich and powerful. In Spanish folktales this often meant the wealthy landowner who gave the poor peasant a job under an unfair contract. In Latin America, the European or North American *gringo*—a word used for all foreigners, although it now refers more and more often to North Americans—has become suitable prey for Pedro. And of course there are stories in which the priest, the schoolmaster, or the mayor is made a fool of. Horses are an indication of a person's wealth, and their riders are thus worthy of Pedro's trickery.

Some of Pedro's exploits will be familiar from stories about other popular and trickster heroes, such as Coyote and Br'er Rabbit, or the Mayan rabbit Juan Tul. Juan Bobo is another Latin American folk hero who shares some of Pedro's adventures. But as his name ("John Fool") suggests, Juan is characterized more by foolishness than by clever trickery. People *take* Urdemales for a fool, and are thus themselves fooled, but Juan Bobo *is* a fool— although sometimes a wise or a lucky one.

The stories in this book are just a sampling of the many that have been told in Latin America and in the southwestern United States. Often the same tale is told in many different places, with only slight variations. A note at the back of the book tells where we have found variations of each story, but these are not the only places where the stories are told.

After all, to quote the storyteller, "They say Pedro Urdemales traveled around the world." Well, at least a lot of it. And he's still traveling. . . .

Clever Little Pedro

When Pedro Urdemales was a boy, he was all alone in the world. He had no home, so he was always wandering from place to place. He had to use his wits to keep himself alive.

One day he was walking down a dusty road in Mexico when he met a priest. "Where does this road go?" asked the priest.

"It doesn't *go* anywhere," answered Pedro. "It always stays in the same place!"

The priest thought that this was a very clever answer. He decided to make Pedro his servant and give him an education.

When Pedro had been living with the priest for a little

while, the priest said to him, "Bring me something that is half I and half not-I."

Pedro went out to the patio and returned with a thorny maguey plant. He peeled the prickly skin off one side and handed the plant to the priest.

The priest took it in his hand, and the thorns pricked his finger. "*Ay!*" he shouted in pain.

"There you have it," said Pedro. "That is the *ay* half. The other side is the not-*ay* half."

Pedro had to work hard, but the priest didn't give him much to eat. When a politician brought the priest a present of some fancy cheeses, he hid them high up in the cupboard where Pedro couldn't reach them.

The next day they were gone. Pedro had eaten them. "But how did you get up there?" asked the priest.

"I used your library," said Pedro. The priest read and re-read every book he owned, trying to find out what Pedro had learned, but he couldn't find anything that told how to get up into high cupboards and steal cheeses. He scratched his head and pondered this question late into the night. But he never did discover that Pedro had indeed used his library: He had piled up all the books and climbed into the cupboard.

Another time, Pedro was asked to serve the priest a roast chicken. The boy was so hungry that, on his way from the kitchen to the table, he ate one of the drumsticks.

"What's this?" asked the priest. "This chicken has only one leg!"

"Of course," said Pedro. And he took the priest out to the chicken house to show him all the chickens sleeping standing on one leg, with the other one tucked up under them.

"Chick, chick, chick, chick," Pedro called. The chickens woke up and put both feet on the ground. "You see," he said to the priest. "You should have called chick, chick, chick, and *your* chicken would have put its leg down too."

"I'll teach you to say chick, chick, chick!" shouted the priest, flying into a rage. Pedro took to his heels, and the priest ran after him, stumbling over his robes. But Pedro was a fast runner, and he got away.

That was not the last time he was fired, chased away, or kicked out. But each time he managed to get something out of it. He had gotten something of an education with the priest. He hadn't learned to read or write, but he'd learned how to get enough to eat. And that was very useful later.

Painted Horses

Pedro soon found a new master. He was another priest, who was very wealthy but no more generous than Pedro's first master. This priest owned a herd of beautiful white horses, and he hired Pedro to clean out their stalls. In return, he gave Pedro a mat to sleep on in the stable, and every day a crust of bread and a few pennies.

One day the priest went away to do some business, and he left Pedro in charge of his horses. The boy spent all his pennies on some paint. He painted brown and black and gray spots on the white horses. Then he brought them into town and sold them for a lot of gold coins. He took the money and went to live far away.

Two years passed. Pedro had had many adventures. He had grown taller, and his voice had changed. He returned

to the town where the priest lived. When he walked past the farm of the man who had bought the painted horses, he saw that the paint had long since been washed off by the rain, and once again the horses were white. That night Pedro crept into the corral, stole the horses, and painted them again.

The next morning when the priest was drinking his coffee, he saw a teenage boy leading a herd of beautiful gray-spotted horses toward his house. There was something vaguely familiar about the boy's face.

"I've heard you're a lover of good horses," said the boy, and with that the flattered priest forgot to wonder where he'd seen him before. Soon he had agreed to buy the herd of "pedigreed grays" for a large sum of money.

After Pedro had gone, the priest got a bucket of water and a brush. He wanted to wash the dust of the road off his new horses.

As the priest stood in the middle of a puddle of gray paint, surrounded by a herd of white horses, the image of Pedro popped into his head. *That* was where he'd seen that face before! That rascal Urdemales had tricked him—and not just once, but twice!

The Golden Partridge

Many, many years later, Pedro Urdemales was walking down a road in Chile without a penny in his pocket. Soon he felt the need to go to the bathroom. Since there wasn't a bathroom to be seen, he squatted beside the road.

Just as he was pulling up his pants, he saw two men riding toward him. Their clothes were embroidered in gold, and they rode beautiful horses. Pedro put down his hat to cover up the mess he had made.

When the two gentlemen rode up, Pedro was holding his hat tight to the ground, as though it might fly away if he let go of it.

"What makes you hold your hat so tight?" asked one of the men.

"I've caught a golden partridge and I don't want it to get away," answered Pedro.

The men looked at the hat. A golden partridge must be worth a lot of money! they thought.

"Maybe you can help me," said Pedro. "I have to go find my brother. He'll help me take this golden bird home. It'll pay my bills for the rest of my life. If I could use one of your horses, I'd be back in a flash. And I know it's a lot to ask—but could you watch the partridge while I'm gone?"

The gentlemen were more than willing to stay and watch over such a valuable treasure. They put Pedro on the back of the better of the two horses and watched him gallop away. "Hah!" they said. "That fool will never see his golden bird again!"

"Is he out of sight yet?" asked the one who was holding down the hat.

"Not yet," said the other. "Wait just a moment . . . yes, now he's gone!"

Both men put their faces down very close to the hat. And then, very, very carefully, one of them put his hand in to grab the golden bird. . . .

The Magic Pot

Pedro Urdemales sold the horse for a great deal of money and went on his way, but it was not long before he had spent all but the last few pennies. He used them to buy a little clay cooking pot and a handful of beans. He found a good spot beside the road, and there he built a fire. Next to the fire he dug a small hole. When the flames had died down, he shoveled the glowing coals into the hole. Then he put his little pot of beans over the coals, so that it seemed to be resting on the ground.

The water in the pot boiled. *"Supper's in my magic pot. Soon I'll eat it, nice and hot!"* sang Pedro as he tapped the pot with a leaf.

Two gentlemen rode up. They were the very same

gentlemen he'd tricked before! They'd gotten themselves another horse.

"Where's my horse, you scoundrel?" one of them demanded.

But Pedro just kept singing: *"Supper's in my magic pot. Soon I'll eat it, nice and hot!"*

The gentlemen stared. "But there's no fire," said one of them.

"That's amazing!" said the other. "How can the water boil?"

Pedro laughed gently. "Of course there's no fire!" he said. "This is a *magic* pot. It *always* boils when I sing to it!" He went on singing dreamily: *"Supper's in my magic pot. Soon I'll eat it, nice and hot!"*

The gentlemen got off their horses and came closer. "I'll give you a hundred gold coins for that pot," one of them offered.

"You must be joking," said Pedro. "It's worth *much* more than that! Now leave me alone and let me eat my supper!"

But the men insisted. They offered two hundred, five hundred, eight hundred, finally a thousand gold coins. At last Pedro sighed. "Well, all right, you win!" he told them.

As soon as the money was in Pedro's hand, he ran off down the road.

The beans were ready, and the gentlemen ate them

all. They stretched and yawned, then picked up the pot to take it home. Underneath, the coals were still glowing faintly.

"That villain!" they shouted. "This time he'll pay with his life!"

The Money Tree

Pedro lived well for a time. When he was down to his last gold coins, he pierced holes in them and hung them on a thornbush. Then he lay down and pretended to be asleep.

Soon the same two gentlemen rode up, looking for him. "There he is!" said one of them. "Sound asleep. This is our chance!" The men dismounted and moved toward Pedro with their knives out. "We'll kill you, you scoundrel. We'll cut your throat and tie your ears to a post!"

Pedro opened his eyes. "And why will you do that?" he asked.

"Because you're the devil who stole our horse. You're the one who made me stick my hand in the muck. You're the one who sold us a piece of junk and called it a magic pot," one gentleman answered, while the other grabbed Pedro by the hair.

But then their eyes caught the glittering gold coins sparkling in the sunshine.

"They're growing on that bush!" whispered one of them.

"If only we had a bush like that, we'd be richer than anyone in the world," breathed the other.

"What is that bush?" the gentlemen asked Pedro.

"Oh, that's just my money tree," said Pedro.

"*Money tree?*"

"Sure," said Pedro. "But I can't tell you about it while you're holding my hair!"

They let go, and Pedro said, "Yes, that's my money tree. Fruit's almost ripe; I'll be harvesting tomorrow, I guess."

"Not if we kill you first," said one gentleman. "How often does it bear fruit?"

"About . . . oh, four, maybe five times a year." Pedro yawned. "If I watered it more, it would bear more often, but I get plenty to cover my needs this way, so why work?"

The men counted on their fingers, and their eyes gleamed with the thought of the golden harvest.

"Listen," they said. "We'll spare your life if you'll let us have your money tree!"

"Oh, no, I wouldn't part with it," answered Pedro.

"What would my life be worth without my little money tree?"

"Oh, come now!" said the gentlemen impatiently. "It's just a silly bush. But we could give you a hundred pesos for it, since it seems to mean so much to you."

"No, no, I don't want to do business with you guys. First you convince me to sell my treasures, and then you come back and complain and threaten me with knives!"

"Five hundred . . ."

"Don't take me for a simpleton!" said Pedro. "You know as well as I do that it'll yield twice that in a year!"

"A thousand," offered the men.

"Not a penny less than five!" said Pedro.

"Done!" said the men.

As soon as the five thousand pesos were in his hand, Pedro ran off down the road.

The next day the two gentlemen harvested the crop of gold coins. They watered the thornbush. They even fertilized it. But it produced no more fruit. After three months, they finally realized that they had been tricked again. But it was too late. Pedro Urdemales might be *anywhere* by now!

Pig Tails in the Swamp

Pedro had enough gold coins to last him for quite a while, so he just kept wandering. By the time he ran out of money, he was on the other side of the Andes Mountains, in Argentina. He got a job on a farm, feeding the pigs and cleaning their pens. One day his boss asked him to take a herd of pigs to market to sell. "Shall I feed them first?" asked Pedro.

"No," replied his stingy boss. "Just give them plenty of water to drink. That way they'll be heavier, and I'll get more money for them."

At the market, Pedro sold all the pigs and pocketed the money—but first he cut off their tails and tucked them away for later.

There was a swamp near the pig farm. Pedro stopped

there on his way home. He took the curly little tails out of his pocket and planted them carefully in the mud.

When Pedro arrived at the farm, he was gasping for breath. "Boss, boss, something awful has happened!" he shouted. "Your pigs have fallen into the swamp! Quick! Help me pull them out!"

The two of them ran down to the swamp, grabbed the pigs' tails, and pulled. But the tails kept coming off in their hands! The boss waded deeper and deeper into the swamp, but all he got was a handful of pig tails. "I'll strangle you! I'll tear you limb from limb!" he shouted, shaking his fist at Pedro.

"But it's not my fault," answered Pedro innocently. "*You're* the one who told me not to feed them! Those poor pigs were starving. They ran into the swamp looking for something to eat. I couldn't hold them back! And then they were so heavy, with all the water you made them drink, that they sank!"

This argument didn't convince the boss. "Out of my sight!" he roared. "Before I skin you!" So Pedro Urdemales galloped away on the boss's horse, his pockets jingling with the money he'd gotten for the pigs.

The Helper Rabbit

There was a time and place, somewhere in Argentina, when Pedro Urdemales had a wife named Teresa. She was as tricky as he was. Between the two of them, they had don José, their wealthy neighbor, at his wits' end. When he swore to kill Pedro for outwitting him one time too many, the couple decided to teach him a lesson.

One morning while Pedro rode into town Teresa prepared an *asado,* which is meat roasted by a fire—and she put plenty of sausages on the grill too.

Soon he came across don José hiding in the bushes by the side of the road. Just as Pedro had expected, his neighbor jumped out and threatened to kill him.

"Spare me! Please!" begged Pedro. "You can't kill a

man who hasn't eaten!" He took a little gray rabbit from inside his jacket.

Don José watched curiously. Was Pedro going to eat that rabbit? he wondered.

But Pedro didn't kill the rabbit. He stroked its ears and whispered, just loudly enough for don José to hear, "Run on home, Little Helper, and tell Teresa we'll have company. Say we'll want a big asado with plenty of sausages." He let the rabbit go, and it hopped off into the fields. "And no dillydallying," called Pedro.

Don José watched the rabbit go. "So, when will this asado be ready?" he asked.

"Oh, don't be impatient," said Pedro. "We can take a little ride, and by the time we get back to my house, the food will be ready." So don José decided to wait to kill his neighbor until after the asado.

"Ah, just in time!" said Teresa when the two men arrived. "That helper of yours told me '*plenty* of sausages,' so I knew there'd be a guest, but I had no idea it would be our dear neighbor don José!"

Don José looked around eagerly. He saw a little gray rabbit tied to a stake, eating grass.

"Good work, Little Helper," said Pedro, patting the rabbit's head.

What don José didn't know was that this was not the same little gray rabbit, but another one just like it.

The three sat down to a delicious asado. Every couple of minutes, don José turned to look at the rabbit. Finally he burst out, "Urdemales, I want to make a deal. I like that little rabbit of yours. If you'll let me have it, I'll spare your life!"

Pedro looked shocked. "I couldn't part with my rabbit!"

"*And* I'll give you this bag of gold. . . ." added don José.

"No, no, and no. And that's final," said Pedro.

"Oh, Pedro, don't let him kill you!" sobbed Teresa, wringing her hands dramatically.

"Well, I do have my wife to think about," said Pedro. "But of course one bag of gold is not enough for that rabbit. Why, there's not another like it in the whole world."

Don José emptied his pockets. He gave them every bit of the gold he had with him. And he left with the little gray rabbit.

The next day don José invited the mayor, the judge, the priest, and all of the other important people of the town to go out riding with him. When they were far from his house, he took the little gray rabbit from his cloak and showed it to the important people. "This rabbit is a wonderful helper!" he told them. "Obedient, quiet, and very clever!"

Then he stroked its ears and whispered to it, just as he had seen Pedro do, "Little Helper, go home and tell my wife to prepare a big asado. Tell her to put on plenty of sausages. We'll have six guests!" He let the rabbit go, and it hopped off into the fields.

All morning long, as they rode around, don José boasted about his helper rabbit. Finally he said, "Well, the asado should be ready by now. Come along to my house and we'll have a great feast."

"What's all this about?" asked don José's wife when she saw him arriving with a group of hungry friends. The table was set for two, and there was nothing to eat but some leftover *locro*. And, of course, there was no little gray rabbit to be seen anywhere.

Don José became the laughingstock of the whole town. And today, when they see him coming, the children still call out, "Hey, don José, where's your helper rabbit?"

Burro Gold

Some years passed, and Pedro the wanderer found himself in Mexico again. Once again, he had an animal helper. But this time it was a burro instead of a rabbit. One day he decided he would have to sell it. He fed it the few gold coins he had left in his pocket.

The next day Pedro and the burro were walking down the road. Pedro heard a clinking sound, and looked down. There, mixed with the burro's manure, were the gold coins.

"Good work," said Pedro to his little burro. "Now we just wait for somebody to come along."

Soon he saw a man riding toward him on a beautiful horse and leading several mules. Pedro got down on the ground and began to separate the coins from the manure.

"What you do?" asked the man.

A gringo, and all the better, thought Pedro. "I'm gathering the coins from my burro's manure."

"Burro manure money?"

"Yes," said Pedro. "He eats grass, and his stomach turns it to gold. I gather a handful of coins like this four or five times every day."

"I buy burro!" said the gringo.

"Oh, no you don't," said Pedro. "I'll never sell my little burro!"

"I give mules, much jewels, much silver," said the gringo.

"Don't make me laugh!" answered Pedro. "What do I want with your mules and silver, when my little burro produces enough gold in a week to load down a dozen mules?"

"I give horse!" said the gringo, dismounting.

"Hmm!" said Pedro. "What good is a horse next to this gold-producing burro? But I *do* like that fancy suit you're wearing. . . . If you gave me that, *and* the horse, *and* the mules, *and* the jewels, *and* the silver, well then maybe . . ."

Before Pedro finished speaking, the gringo had stripped down to his underwear.

"Farewell, my friend!" called Pedro as he rode away

on the gringo's horse, leading his mules and wearing his suit. Looking back, he saw the gringo standing in his underwear, patting the little burro on its head and kissing its nose.

Pedro and the Devil

The roads led Pedro Urdemales west, then north, then south again. One day, in Chile, he came face to face with the Devil, who happened to be walking down the same road. The Devil had been hearing of Pedro's exploits for a long time.

"Just the man I've been looking for!" cried the Devil. "You think you're so clever? Well, let's see if you can beat the Devil! I challenge you to a contest!"

"What's the prize?" asked Pedro.

"If you win, you get a coffer full of gold that's buried in the graveyard. If I win, I get your soul!"

"All right," said Pedro.

"The first contest will be stone throwing. We'll meet

tomorrow by the sea. The one who can throw the stone farther wins."

Early the next morning, Pedro and the Devil met beside the sea. Pedro, of course, had something up his sleeve.

The Devil threw first. He threw his stone far out to sea, and it landed in the water with a splash.

Then it was Pedro's turn. But what he had up his sleeve was a quail, and it was this bird, and not the stone, that he threw into the air. It flew far, far away, until neither Pedro nor the Devil could see it anymore.

The Devil didn't know that Pedro's stone was really a bird, so he had to admit that Pedro had won the first contest.

"But," said the Devil, "we're going to have another contest. We'll see who can drive his fist deeper into a tree trunk. We'll do it right here, tomorrow." They chose a big, solid tree, and agreed to meet the next morning.

That night Pedro made a deep hole in one side of the tree and carefully covered it with a thin layer of bark, so that the tree looked exactly as it had before.

The next morning, the Devil was again the first to try. He got a running start from ten feet away, and he punched the tree so hard that his fist went in all the way up to the wrist.

Then it was Pedro's turn. He backed up and got a running start from ten feet away on the other side of the tree. He punched the tree just where he'd made the hole the night before. *His* arm went right through that tree! So Pedro won the second contest, too.

"All right, all right, you're strong," the Devil admitted. "But now we're going to try at business. You can't beat the Devil at business!" He rubbed his hands together. "Whoever does better wins the whole contest."

They decided to grow vegetables. "Let's grow potatoes," said Pedro. "You can pick what grows above the ground, and I'll pick what grows underground." This seemed like a good deal to the Devil.

When it was time to harvest their crop, the Devil picked first. He picked all the leaves and stems. Then it was Pedro's turn. He dug up the potatoes. He had piles and piles of potatoes, and he sold them for a lot of money.

"But next time it's my turn to harvest what grows underground!" said the Devil.

"Fair enough," said Pedro. "We can plant wheat."

So they planted wheat. The Devil watched the stalks grow taller and taller, and he imagined the great big vegetables underground that would be his share. At the end of the summer, Pedro picked the grain from aboveground.

"So, you have some grass and seeds," said the Devil. "But now I'll get the food!" He dug and scratched in the soil, but all he found were scraggly roots.

"Well, neither of us got anything this time," he said.

But Pedro took his wheat to the mill, ground it into flour, and sold it for a lot of money.

When the Devil saw this, he realized that he had better stop before he lost even more than just gold coins. So he grudgingly admitted that Pedro had won. That night they went to the graveyard and dug up the coffer of gold. Pedro carried it off, whistling cheerfully, and the Devil went away in a terrible mood.

That was Pedro Urdemales: more devil than the Devil himself!

Pedro Fools the Gringo

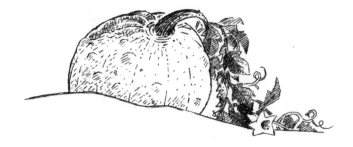

Although Pedro was growing old, there were still plenty of tricks he could play.

As he was walking down a road somewhere in Chile, he noticed an enormous round squash growing in a field. He picked it, and was walking along carrying it in his arms when he met a rich gringo riding an excellent horse.

"What is that you've got there, my good fellow?" asked the gringo, looking down his nose at Pedro.

"It's a mare's egg," answered Pedro. "A racing colt will soon hatch from it."

"Well, well, we're both in luck then," said the gringo. "I happen to know a lot about horses, and lately I've been

thinking I'd love to raise a colt and train it to be the greatest racehorse ever. And then along you come with just what I need! Sell me that egg!"

"Oh, no," said Pedro. "I don't want to sell this egg just before it hatches."

But the gringo was determined that Pedro would not deny him this opportunity to become a great horse breeder, and so after much bargaining he was able to convince him to sell the precious egg for a large sum of money.

After pocketing the money, Pedro gently placed the squash on the gringo's saddle. "Take care of that egg," he warned. "You don't want to break it and lose your colt."

The gringo continued on his way, but he didn't get very far. The ground was rough, and as he rode along a narrow path on a hillside, his horse stumbled on a loose rock. The gringo let go of the mare's egg for just a second, and it fell from his saddle.

"Stop!" shouted the gringo as his treasure went rolling down the hill.

At the bottom of the hill was a stump surrounded by brambles. A fox was sleeping in the brambles. The squash crashed into the stump and split open. The fox jumped up, frightened, and ran away as fast as it could.

"My racing colt! My racing colt!" cried the gringo.

He spurred his horse and took off after the fox. "What a fast colt it is! Help me catch my colt!" he cried. But Pedro laughed and ran off in the opposite direction.

"Good-bye to Your Machetes . . ."

Pedro Urdemales had played tricks on a lot of people, and at last, in Guatemala, some of them caught up with him. They came on horseback, armed with whips and pistols, machetes and knives, and swore that *this* time it would be the end of Pedro Urdemales.

They tied him up, put him into a big sack, and carried him to the edge of a deep ravine with a river at the bottom. But before throwing him into the river, they decided to have a bite to eat. Then they all lay down to take a siesta.

Inside the sack, Pedro freed himself from the ropes. When everyone was snoring, he crawled out. He gathered together all the whips, machetes, pistols, and knives, and he put them into the sack. He took the saddles and bridles

and spurs from their horses and put them into the sack too. Then he tied it shut again and hid among some rocks.

Soon the sleepers awoke. They stretched and yawned. "The time has come!" they said triumphantly. They lifted the heavy sack, swung it back and forth a couple of times, and then threw it far out over the cliff and into the river.

"Good-bye, Pedro Urdemales," they called after it, "and good riddance!"

But as the sack hit the water, the people heard an echo coming from the rocks above them: "Good-bye to your machetes and pistols and whips! Good-bye to your saddles and bridles!"

They had not gotten rid of Pedro Urdemales!

Pedro Goes to Heaven

After a long life of travel and tricks, Pedro Urdemales died. He wanted to go to Heaven, of course, but San Pedro refused to let him in the gate. "You haven't been good enough," he said.

"Oh, but my dear namesake," pleaded Pedro, "just a little tiny peek . . ."

San Pedro unlocked the gate and opened it just a crack, and Pedro stuck his nose in. Then San Pedro tried to close the gate. "Ouch!" said Pedro. "You're squashing my nose! Let me take it out!"

San Pedro loosened his hold on the gate just a bit, and Pedro, instead of taking his nose out, stuck his whole head inside. "Ow! You're squashing my head!" he cried.

San Pedro let go of the door for just a second, and

Pedro Urdemales gave a shove and was head and shoulders inside the gates. "Now my good part is in Heaven," he said, "and my bad part is outside."

San Pedro leaned with all his weight on the gate to keep it closed.

Pedro Urdemales stayed stuck there for a long time. Finally San Pedro got tired of not being able to use his gate. He let go, and Pedro Urdemales tumbled in. But San Pedro knew that if Urdemales were free to wander around Heaven, there would be no more peace. So, to protect himself from Pedro's tricks, he said, "You will become a stone, and stay perfectly still, right there beside the gate."

"At least let me look around," pleaded Pedro. "Let me be a stone—but with eyes." San Pedro decided that could

do no harm, and so he made him into a stone with eyes.

And that is how Pedro Urdemales came to be a stone, watching and watching, beside the gates of Heaven.

Where the Stories Come From

CLEVER LITTLE PEDRO Mexico. One-legged chicken also found in Guatemala and in Puerto Rico (Juan Bobo).
Sources: Paredes; Hernández.

PAINTED HORSES Mexico.
Source: Toor.

THE GOLDEN PARTRIDGE Chile, Argentina, Bolivia (Pedro Urdimalis), Guatemala, Puerto Rico (Juan Bobo), Mexico, and New Mexico.
Sources: Pino-Saavedra, 1967; Sexton; Roldán; Recinos; Wheeler.

THE MAGIC POT Chile, Argentina, Mexico, and Guatemala (Pedro Tecomate).
Sources: Pino-Saavedra, 1967; Shaw; Roldán; Paredes.

THE MONEY TREE Chile, Mexico, and Guatemala.
Sources: Pino-Saavedra, 1967; Paredes; Toor.

PIG TAILS IN THE SWAMP Chile, Mexico, Argentina, Guatemala, and Spain.
Sources: Roldán; Pino-Saavedra, 1967; Paredes; Toor.

THE HELPER RABBIT Argentina; also found in Spain as a "Los dos compadres" story.
Sources: Roldán; Espinosa, 1923.

BURRO GOLD Mexico, Guatemala, and Spain.
Sources: Paredes; Espinosa, 1923; Recinos.

PEDRO AND THE DEVIL Variations found in Chile, Argentina, and Spain.
Sources: Pino-Saavedra, 1988; Roldán; Espinosa, 1923.

PEDRO FOOLS THE GRINGO Chile.
Source: Pino-Saavedra, 1967.

"GOOD-BYE TO YOUR MACHETES . . ." Chile, Mexico, Guatemala, and Spain.
Sources: Toor; Pino-Saavedra, 1967; Shaw; Espinosa, 1923; Recinos.

PEDRO GOES TO HEAVEN Guatemala, Chile, Mexico, and Argentina.
Sources: Recinos; Wheeler; Pino-Saavedra, 1967.

Bibliography

Aramburu, Julio. *Las hazañas de Pedro Urdemales.* Buenos Aires: Librería El Ateneo, 1949.

Cervantes, Miguel. *Comedia famosa de Pedro de Urdemalas.* New York: Las Americas Publishing Co., 1966.

Coluccio, Félix, and Marta Isabel Coluccio. *Presencia del diablo en la tradición oral de Iberoamérica.* Buenos Aires: Ediciones Culturales Argentinas, 1987.

Espinosa, Aurelio. *Cuentos populares españoles.* Stanford, California: Stanford University Press, 1923.

———. "New-Mexican Spanish Folk-Lore." *Journal of American Folk-Lore.* Vol. 27 (1914): 119–134.

Hernández, Roberto. *Nuevos cuentos de Juan Bobo.* San Juan, Puerto Rico: Editorial Yaurel, 1987.

Mason, J. Alden. "Folk-Tales of the Tepecanos." *Journal of American Folk-Lore.* Vol. 27 (1914): 166–171, 189–199.

Paredes, Americo. *Folktales of Mexico.* Chicago: University of Chicago Press, 1970.

Paredes-Candia, Antonio. *Cuentos populares bolivianos.* La Paz: Librería-Editorial Popular, 1984.

Pino-Saavedra, Yolando. *Cuentos mapuches de Chile.* Santiago de Chile: Editorial Universitaria, 1988.

———. *Folktales of Chile.* Chicago: University of Chicago Press, 1967.

Recinos, Adrián. "Cuentos populares de Guatemala." *Journal of American Folk-Lore,* Vol. 31 (1918): 472–487.

Roldán, Gustavo. *Cuentos de Pedro Urdemales.* Buenos Aires: Ediciones Culturales Argentinas, 1986.

Shaw, Mary, ed. *According to Our Ancestors: Folk Texts from Guatemala and Honduras.* Norman: Summer Institute of Linguistics of the University of Oklahoma, 1971.

Toor, Frances. *A Treasury of Mexican Folkways.* New York: Crown, 1947.

Wheeler, Howard T. *Tales from Jalisco, Mexico.* Philadelphia: Memoirs of the American Folk-Lore Society, 1943.